BUNNY

Christina Schwabauer

ISBN 978-1-63814-927-9 (Paperback)
ISBN 978-1-63814-950-7 (Hardcover)
ISBN 978-1-63814-949-1 (Digital)

Covenant Books, Inc.
11661 Hwy 707
Murrells Inlet, SC 29576
www.covenantbooks.com

I am extremely blessed and thankful for my husband, Michael. You always stand by me, support me, and have confidence in me when I cannot find it for myself. You always overlook my flaws and only see my potential. Thank you for being God's perfect man for me!

Thank you, Jennifer, for bringing Bunny and Jessica to life with your creative beauty.

For my grandchildren

Every day was an adventure for Bunny and Jessica.

What would today hold for them?

Bunny wanted to play, but Jessica was still sleeping. She would have to wait.

It seemed like it was taking forever.

Finally, it was time to have some fun. Bunny loved
Jessica and loved playing anything with her.

They were just finishing up breakfast. Jessica had shared it with Bunny just like every day.

Bunny was excited to see what she and Jessica would do today.

Jessica picked up Bunny gently and gave her a snuggle.

In Jessica's room, she sat Bunny down and made her comfy, then grabbed a book. Bunny loved it when she read stories to her.

By lunch time, Bunny had also played dress-up, built a fort, baked a souffle, and colored pretty pony pictures.

Lunch was an apple and peanut butter sandwich. Yum!

Bunny could hardly wait to see what fun was going to happen next.

Jessica grabbed her favorite blanket, and the two of them went outside. They had been smelling the flowers and picking some for Mom's table too.

Jessica had flowers in her hair. Bunny even had flowers to wear around her neck and behind her ears.

They lay back on the blanket. Looking up at the clouds, you could find all kinds of fun things, a plane, a teddy bear, a rainbow, a princess riding her pony, a dragonfly, and a snake!

But now Jessica had another great idea.

Bunny loved riding in Jessica's basket while she rode her bike. They would go so fast up and down the driveway that Bunny's ears would flop back in the wind.

Her heart was racing, and Jessica had a huge smile on her face. Bunny knew she was almost flying!

Outside was always so much fun, but it had started to sprinkle, and Mom was calling them to come in. Jessica threw Bunny up on her shoulders and skipped into the house.

Jessica got down on the floor with Bunny on her back and started to *neigh* and gallop around the living room. Bunny flopped back and forth holding on to the bucking bronco. Oh, how Bunny loved playing pony!

Mom told them to wash up for dinner. Jessica shut the bathroom light off, and they danced and twirled like ballerinas all the way to the table.

Jessica sat Bunny on a pile of books right next to her at the table so Bunny could see. Spaghetti! Jessica and Bunny's favorite! Which meant they got to take a bath after dinner. What fun!

The tub was full of bubbles. Bunny had been wiped off and was sitting on the side of the tub. Jessica was playing with her sea friends, starfish, whale, walrus, and stingray. They were riding the bubbles and splashing around.

Bunny was just happy that Jessica was having fun. She loved to hear Jessica laugh and giggle.

After the bath, they put on their PJs, grabbed Jessica's favorite blanket, and climbed up into the chair with Mom to hear a story. Tonight's story was about a bunny and her friends playing in a garden.

After hugs and kisses, they climbed into bed and said their prayers and thanked God for their day. They snuggled in together, thinking about tomorrow and another great adventure!

God made the birdies, rainbows, flowers, and you. Ask Him to live in your heart. He will always be with you!

About the Illustrator

Award-winning artist Jennifer Ross has been creating since she was very little. Many years later, graduating from the University of Michigan with a fine arts degree, she got married and moved to the UP with her husband and young baby girl. After six years, and another baby girl, she and her family moved to lower Michigan and quickly got involved in the local art center. Since then, she has been in two solo shows, taught art to local senior citizens, and been involved with many group shows around mid-Michigan.

About the Author

Christina Schwabauer began writing her first children's book after remembering the joy of watching her daughter Jessica and Bunny play for hours together and knew others would enjoy them too.

She married the perfect man almost twenty-four years ago and has been blessed with being a stay-at-home mom to their four wonderful children.

Christina relies daily on her faith in God and enjoys coffee dates with friends, going camping, and her two beautiful grandbabies.

CPSIA information can be obtained
at www.ICGtesting.com
Printed in the USA
BVHW022232241121
622496BV00004B/92